TOM AND JERRY

TOM and JERRY
MEET MR. FINGERS

by

Carl Fallberg

A WHITMAN BOOK
Western Publishing Company, Inc.
Racine, Wisconsin

© 1967 by Metro-Goldwyn-Mayer Inc.
All rights reserved.

Produced in U.S.A. by
Western Publishing Company, Inc.

WHITMAN and BIG LITTLE BOOK
are registered trademarks of
Western Publishing Company, Inc.

No part of this book may be reproduced
or copied in any form without written
permission from the publisher.

CONTENTS

CHAPTER		PAGE
1	Enter F.E.L.I.N.E.	9
2	Runaway Tire	27
3	Mr. Fingers' Secret	37
4	A Persistent Cat	59
5	Jerry to the Rescue	67
6	The Saboteur's Schedule	89
7	A Sticky Situation	113
8	A Plot is Hatched	133
9	F.E.L.I.N.E. Fiasco	147
10	Trestle Trouble	165
11	Daffodil Diversion	195
12	A Messy Missile	229
13	A New Start	243

A Favorite Program

CHAPTER 1

ENTER F.E.L.I.N.E.

Tom and Jerry were watching their favorite TV program, "Secret Agent 6⅞, the Nemesis of the Underworld."

"Hey, Tom, look!" cried Jerry. "The crooks have thrown Agent Six and Seven-Eighths out of a plane at fifty thousand feet without any oxygen or a parachute!"

"Aw, don't worry about Agent Six and Seven-Eighths," replied Tom. "He'll get out of this mess like he always does!"

"I sure hope so!" said Jerry. "I'd hate to lose my favorite TV hero!"

As they watched, it seemed hopeless. Agent $6\frac{7}{8}$ plunged down and down. How could he survive without oxygen, let alone a parachute?

But Jerry failed to reckon with Agent $6\frac{7}{8}$'s resourcefulness. All of a sudden he swooped upward.

"See? What did I tell you!" said

A TV Secret Agent

Tom. "He'll get out of it!"

Agent 6⅞ had a pair of trick shoes with powerful jets in the heels that enabled him to zoom around in the air. Also, he had tremendous lung capacity, which enabled him to get oxygen from a minimum amount of air. In no time he'd overtaken the plane, battered his way in, and subdued the crooks.

"There! He did it again!" said Tom. "No crooks in the world can stand up against Secret Agent Six and Seven-Eighths!"

"I guess you're right!" agreed

"He Did It Again!"

Jerry with a sigh of relief.

"I'd sure like to be an agent like Six and Seven-Eighths," mused Tom. "What an exciting life that would be!"

Jerry had to laugh. "I think you'd make a better dogcatcher than secret agent."

Tom bristled. "Never mind the insults!" he snapped. "Someday I'll show you whether I can be a secret agent or not!"

"That'll be the day!" said Jerry.

Just then the commercial came on.

Friendly Argument

"Guess I'll snooze through this," Tom yawned. "Commercials bore me."

The commercial had to do with a cereal called Bombsie Wombsies, which the sponsor claimed was the favorite food of Agent $6\tfrac{7}{8}$. In each package was an Instant Trench Coat like $6\tfrac{7}{8}$ wore. You made it by simply adding water. Tom perked up.

"That's for me!" he said. "There's a package of Bombsie Wombsies in the kitchen! I'll be a secret agent yet!" He went to get

Bombsie Wombsies

the cereal and to make his trench coat.

Just then the program was interrupted by an important news bulletin. Ten new military jets had been sabotaged. Their wings had been crushed as though by gigantic pliers.

The announcer hinted darkly that it looked like the work of a foreign agent. Last week a section of a freeway had been torn up by the same unknown force. They had no clues as to who, or what, was doing the damage.

Special News Bulletin!

"Well, that's where I come in!" announced Tom. "Just call me F.E.L.I.N.E."

"What in the world does F.E.L.I.N.E. stand for?" Jerry asked.

"Fearless Enforcer of the Law with Indomitable and Never-Ending Energy!" replied Tom, wrapping his trench coat around him.

"Huh!" snorted Jerry. "That'd be F.E.O.T.L.W.I.A.N.E.E."

"Don't get technical!" snapped Tom. "Let's get on with it! You can be my assistant!"

"Thanks a lot!" said Jerry. "And

"Just Call Me F.E.L.I.N.E."

I can see where you *do* need help!"

"Now," continued Tom, pacing around the room. "Let's see where this vicious saboteur might strike next! The city dump, perhaps?"

Just then a distant locomotive whistle sounded.

"Or the railroad!" said Jerry.

"The railroad! Of course!" exclaimed Tom. "I'm sure glad I thought of that! It's a natural for a vicious foreign agent to destroy!"

"And don't forget places like dams and bridges," remarked Jerry.

Wondering Where to Start

"Don't worry!" assured Tom. "I'll take care of all those places! No saboteur is going to get away with anything when F.E.L.I.N.E. is on the job."

"I'll Be Ready!"

A Blowout

CHAPTER 2

RUNAWAY TIRE

Driving determinedly toward the railroad, Tom envisioned himself catching the saboteur and being proclaimed a hero. The sudden bang of a blowing tire brought him back to reality.

"Shucks!" muttered Tom, bringing the car to a stop. "I was hoping to catch that saboteur in the act! This is going to delay me!"

As they struggled to lift the spare from the trunk, Tom tripped over his trench coat. He lost his grip on the tire and it landed on his foot.

"OUCH!" Tom yelped, grabbing his injured toes. He watched in amazement as the tire started rolling down the hill toward a dammed-up reservoir. Suddenly moved to action, Tom and Jerry started out in hot pursuit.

To their horror, they saw an old man crossing the dam—and the tire

"Ouch!"

was heading straight for him!

"Look out!" they yelled, but too late. The rolling tire bumped into the man and knocked him into the water.

They lost no time in pulling him out, apologizing all the while. However, the man just muttered something and continued across the dam to the other side.

Then Jerry noticed that the old man had dropped his watch. It was an elaborate device, full of complicated-looking dials. He picked it up and showed it to Tom.

An Elaborate Watch

Tom thought it might be a valuable heirloom and yelled at the old man to stop. But apparently he was hard of hearing, for he continued across the dam and up the road to a small sports car. He got in and drove off.

Jerry decided it was strange that an old man would drive such a car and mentioned that fact to Tom. However, Tom paid no attention because he was busy retrieving the runaway tire from the water and dragging it back up the hill to the car.

The Old Man Drives Off

Having changed the tire, Tom announced that they would follow the road the old man had taken and attempt to return his watch.

"We'll Follow Him!"

A Locked Gate

CHAPTER 3

MR. FINGERS' SECRET

The road led up to a mansion set high on a hill, surrounded by a high iron fence with a locked gate.

They rang the bell but got no response.

"Let's just leave the watch here and forget it," said Tom.

"No," replied Jerry, "I think I

can squeeze through the gate and unlock it from the inside."

Jerry slipped between the bars, opened the gate, and then, with Tom, proceeded up the walk to the front door.

Tom, watch in hand, was just about to push the doorbell when the door opened and a huge butler almost seven feet tall grabbed him and yanked him inside.

The butler had failed to notice tiny Jerry, who had been standing behind Tom. The door had slammed before Jerry could utter a sound.

Yanked In

Jerry was flabbergasted. Because Tom had been swooped inside so rapidly, he reasoned, there must be something going on in the place. But what? And what could he do?

Then Jerry noticed an open window high on the side of the house. He decided to climb up and see if he could determine what was going on inside.

It took some doing, but Jerry finally made it up to the window ledge. He peered inside.

Jerry saw a large room with a big desk at one end. Behind the desk

Jerry Peers Inside

sat the old man they had seen at the reservoir. He was in the process of taking off his beard, revealing himself as a totally different person.

Just then the butler, carrying Tom, entered and dumped his prisoner in front of the man at the desk.

"Well, well! Who have we here?" asked the man. "My friend from the dam! What are you doing here?"

"I—I just wanted to return your watch," Tom stammered.

"And just how did you get past the locked gate?" the man asked.

"Well, Who Have We Here?"

Tom was in a quandary. He didn't want to let them know about Jerry, so he said nothing.

"Won't talk, eh?" said the man. "Well, I don't mind. Let me introduce myself. I'm Mr. Fingers! And do you know why they call me that? Let me show you!"

He picked up one of the many steel ball bearings lying on his desk and squeezed it flat between his fingers as though it were made of clay.

Tom gulped. He realized he was face to face with something very

"I'm Mr. Fingers!"

sinister and frightening.

"Now that you know my secret," growled Mr. Fingers, "you'll have to stay here." He motioned to the huge butler. "Lock him up securely, Slurk!"

The giant butler collared poor Tom, marched him down a long hall, and threw him into a dungeon-like room.

At this point Tom wasn't so sure he wanted to be a secret agent. He tried to think what $6\frac{7}{8}$ would do in a case like this, but couldn't think of a thing.

To the Dungeon

Meanwhile, Jerry had quietly crept through the window and past Mr. Fingers, who failed to notice him because he was busy flattening ball bearings. Reaching the hall, Jerry had silently followed Tom and the butler.

Jerry watched the butler put the key to the dungeon in his pocket. Then he waited while the butler sat down to read the paper. Eventually Slurk dozed and Jerry managed to sneak the key out of his pocket.

However, when Jerry got to the

Slurk Dozes

door there was the problem of getting up to the lock. Since Jerry was only six inches tall and the lock was four feet from the floor, this looked like quite a problem. Finally, with great effort, he managed to push a chair over to the door, climb up, insert the key, and unlock the door.

Tom was overjoyed at being released. Now, however, there was the problem of getting out of the building.

Sneaking down the hall, they heard voices. They hid behind a suit of armor and listened. They

They Hide and Listen

recognized the voices of Mr. Fingers and his butler.

"Slurk, I have a little, ah, job to do today, so take care of things here," Mr. Fingers said.

"Yes, sir," replied Slurk.

"And take special care of our guest!" instructed Mr. Fingers.

"Don't worry, sir, I will!" said Slurk ominously.

The door slammed.

Jerry looked at Tom. "We'd better tell the police!" he whispered.

Tom agreed.

They had to wait until Slurk was

Mr. Fingers Leaves

again dozing in his chair before they could sneak out.

They were soon in Tom's car and hurrying down the road.

"What do you suppose this Mr. Fingers character is up to?" wondered Tom.

"I'm not sure," replied Jerry. "But I wouldn't be at all surprised if he had something to do with all this sabotage stuff!"

"Say," said Tom as though he had thought of the idea all by himself, "I'll bet he's the saboteur! With his strong fingers, he could

Tom and Jerry Escape

break airplane wings like nothing!"

"Sure," added Jerry. "And even rip up freeways!"

"Well, I'll bet Chief McMinion will be glad to hear about this," said Tom as he parked the car in front of the police station.

The Police Station

"I'm a Secret Agent!"

CHAPTER 4

A PERSISTENT CAT

"What can I do for you?" asked the chief as Tom and Jerry burst into his office.

"I'm a secret agent," Tom announced grandly. "F.E.L.I.N.E., to be exact. And I think I have the answer to all this sabotage that's been going on!"

"Doesn't everybody?" growled the chief. "What's *your* theory?"

Tom went on to explain what had happened. He got things a bit mixed up. The chief was confused, but he listened patiently while Tom rambled on. Finally his patience was exhausted.

"Look!" he snapped. "Every Tom, Dick, and Harry imagines himself as a secret agent these days. The man you mentioned is a respected citizen named J. Hamhock Hamstrung! Every year he donates daffodils to be planted around

Impatient Chief

the city reservoir!"

"I—I didn't know that!" replied Tom.

"You know now!" said the chief. "So go home and hang up your trench coat!"

Tom wasn't to be discouraged so easily. As they walked back to the car he told Jerry his plans.

"I don't know about you," he said, "but I'm going back to that place and see what Mr. Fingers is really up to!"

Jerry sighed. "Maybe the chief is right, Tom. Maybe it would be

Back to the Car

a wild-goose chase."

"Nevertheless, I'm not going to give up!" declared Tom. "We secret agents don't give up easily!"

Jerry sighed again. He'd have to go along with the gag, if only to keep Tom out of trouble.

"I'm Not Giving Up!"

Cautious Approach

CHAPTER 5

JERRY TO THE RESCUE

They reached the Hamstrung residence and, after parking the car out of sight, proceeded to the house. Again Jerry unlocked the gate and they cautiously sneaked in.

"How do we get into the house? I just can't go up and ring the bell like I did before!" said Tom.

"Through a window!" said Jerry.

But while crossing the lawn, Tom tripped over a wire. Jerry, being small, walked under it. Tom fell flat on his face and was stunned. Almost immediately there was a loud clanging of bells and howling of sirens. Tom had touched off the alarm system!

"Run for it, Tom!" Jerry yelled.

Tom was too dazed to respond. Jerry tried to drag him to the gate, but Tom was too heavy. Then, to

Tom Trips the Alarm

Jerry's horror, he heard the front door of the house open.

"Who's there?" It was the voice of Slurk, the butler.

In desperation Jerry tried to revive Tom with spray from a nearby garden hose.

"Who's there?" again demanded Slurk. "Whoever you are, come out with your hands up!" Carrying a gun, Slurk lunged into sight.

"Tom! Wake up and let's get out of here!" Jerry shouted in Tom's ear.

"So there you are!" yelled Slurk

Jerry Tries to Revive Tom

as he started toward them, gun aimed.

This was indeed a desperate moment. Jerry was frantic. He must find a way to stop Slurk, who was coming closer and closer.

All of a sudden he had an inspiration. The garden hose! Grabbing it, he aimed the nozzle right at Slurk, catching him full in the face with a stream of water.

"Ah! Blub!" gasped Slurk as he slipped and fell.

At that moment Tom came to and groggily got to his feet.

Jerry's Aim Is Good

"Run for the gate!" cried Jerry.

Tom started to run, but not for the gate—instead he ran for the house!

"Tom!" screamed Jerry. "You're going the wrong way!"

"No, he's not!" snarled Slurk, getting to his feet and taking off after poor Tom. In no time he had Tom firmly by the collar.

"I don't know how you got out," said Slurk, "but you won't get out again! Maybe your little friend had something to do with it! I'd better get him, too!"

Slurk Pursues Tom

He made a grab for Jerry, who easily eluded him and dashed into the bushes.

"I'll take care of you later!" growled Slurk as he carried Tom into the house.

Jerry watched helplessly from the safety of the bushes. He was sure of one thing—Slurk would be more careful with the key this time. How on earth would he find a way to get Tom free again?

When Jerry tried to get back into the house through the window he had used before, he found it locked.

Jerry Watches Helplessly

He walked all around the house but found no more open windows. Slurk had evidently taken all possible precautions.

Jerry thought and thought. Going to the police was out, since Chief McMinion already thought that Tom was some kind of a nut. The only thing he could do was march right in the front door.

Jerry looked around until he found a long stick. Then he went around to the front door and poked at the doorbell with the stick. He heard a distant ring. After a pause

Jerry Solves His Problem

the door was cautiously opened by Slurk.

"Who's there?" the butler demanded.

Unfortunately the door wasn't opened far enough for Jerry to squeeze through. He kept silent.

"Who's there?" Slurk asked again, opening the door a little wider.

Jerry dashed between Slurk's huge feet and into the house. Inside, he ducked behind a chair leg as Slurk closed the door.

"I could have sworn I heard the

Jerry Dashes In

bell ring!" he muttered. "I must need a vacation!"

Jerry was about to go down to the dungeon, where he felt sure Tom was languishing, when he heard the sound of a door opening. Jerry peered out and saw Mr. Fingers enter.

"Did you ring the bell a minute ago, sir?" asked Slurk.

"Why in blazes should I do that?" Mr. Fingers growled. "You know I have a key of my own!"

"Sorry, sir," Slurk apologized. "I guess I was hearing things."

Mr. Fingers Returns

Mr. Fingers went to his desk, sat down, and squeezed a few ball bearings.

"I've had a most productive day," Mr. Fingers announced. "I bent a few rails at the railroad yards."

"Good, sir," commented Slurk. "What's next on your schedule?"

"Oh, the dam, perhaps," replied Mr. Fingers.

Jerry gasped. It was true, then, that Mr. Fingers was the mysterious saboteur. Now there was all the more reason to get Tom out of his

Finger Exercises

cell, and out of this house!

Mr. Fingers yawned. "I've had a very busy day. I think I'll take a nap."

"Very good, sir," said Slurk. He didn't tell Mr. Fingers that Tom had escaped once. As long as he was back in custody, what did it matter?

As soon as Mr. Fingers and Slurk left the room Jerry hurried to the dungeon.

Down to the Dungeon

"Tom! It's Me! Jerry!"

CHAPTER 6

THE SABOTEUR'S SCHEDULE

On his way to the dungeon, Jerry realized that getting Tom out this time wouldn't be any cinch. He couldn't count on picking Slurk's pocket as he had done before.

Reaching the dungeon, he whispered, "Tom! It's me! Jerry!"

The only sound from within was

a steady gentle snoring.

"For heaven's sake," Jerry said to himself. "He's fallen asleep!"

Jerry rapped on the door, and to his surprise it swung open. Incredibly enough, Slurk had forgotten to lock it. This was certainly a break.

He tapped Tom lightly and he awoke with a start.

"Wh-where am I?" he faltered sleepily.

"In Mr. Fingers' dungeon!" answered Jerry. "Come on! We've got to get out of here fast! You've got

Jerry Wakes Tom

to pull yourself together!"

Tom pulled himself together and soon they were back upstairs.

Slurk was snoozing in a chair. They carefully tiptoed toward the front door.

Tom was about to open the door when Jerry remembered something. Slurk had mentioned a schedule of sabotage. Maybe it was on Mr. Fingers' desk.

Jerry hopped up on the desk and scrambled through the papers. His searching eyes discovered a sheet of paper with ominous notations.

A Hasty Search

Jet planes √
Freeway √
Railroad yards √
Railroad bridge
Dam

Jerry knew he had found Mr. Fingers' schedule. The two unchecked items on the list, the railroad bridge and the dam, meant that Mr. Fingers had not yet sabotaged them.

"Look at this, Tom!" he exclaimed.

"What is it?" asked Tom.

"Shh! Not so loud!" said Jerry.

The Saboteur's Schedule

"You might wake Slurk!"

"Oh, don't worry about Slurk," answered Tom. "From the snoring he's doing, it would take a bomb to wake him. Let's see that!" He reached for the paper.

"See what I mean?" asked Jerry. "Here's a complete timetable of Mr. Fingers' sabotage plans. If we show *this* to Chief McMinion, maybe then he'll take us seriously!"

"Agreed! Let's go!" said Tom.

They started for the door, but in his haste Tom tripped over his trench coat and fell practically in

"Let's Go!"

the sleeping Slurk's lap.

Slurk awoke with a start to see Tom staring him in the face. He leaped out of his chair and made a grab for Tom, who ducked just in time.

Slurk lost his balance and crashed into a suit of armor, sending it flying in all directions with a tremendous clatter.

Tom and Jerry lost no time in getting out of the house. They had managed to get through the gate and to their car when Tom noticed that he'd lost the piece of paper

Slurk Stumbles

on which Mr. Fingers' sabotage schedule was written. He stopped.

"I've got to go back for it!" he said. "Otherwise Chief McMinion will never believe me!"

"Don't be silly!" said Jerry. "If you go back they'll nab you for sure!"

"What'll we do?" asked Tom.

"At least we know who's behind all of this stuff!" replied Jerry. "The important thing right now is to get out of here! It won't take Mr. Fingers long to find out you've escaped."

"What'll We Do?"

"I'm with you!" said Tom as he started the car. "But I still think we should tell Chief McMinion what we found. *Maybe* he'll believe us."

"I doubt it," replied Jerry. "Don't forget, you didn't make a very good impression the last time you saw him."

"Let's try, anyway," Tom said.

Meanwhile, back at the house, Slurk was disentangling himself from the armor he'd crashed into. A very angry Mr. Fingers had

Mr. Fingers Finds Slurk

just come into the room.

"What's all this racket about?" he demanded. "I was napping!"

Slurk gulped. He hated to admit that Tom had again escaped.

"I'm afraid, sir, that our prisoner has escaped. I—I don't know how—" Slurk stammered timorously.

Deep in thought, Mr. Fingers paced about the room.

"I think we're dealing with a very clever secret agent," he said. "I thought he was a complete idiot, but it seems I was wrong!"

Deep in Thought

"What's to be done, sir?" asked Slurk.

"The first thing we must do is eliminate that cat!" replied Mr. Fingers.

"And how do you propose to do that?" asked Slurk.

"Here's the answer!" Mr. Fingers said, holding up a piece of paper. "I got his name and address from the registration slip on his car, which he had clumsily hidden in the bushes."

He handed the paper to Slurk.

"Now, here's what I want you to

"Here's the Answer!"

do," he continued. "Tomorrow you will go to see that cat and say that you have some important information for him. Tell him to meet you the next day at the old railroad bridge on the north side of town at nine o'clock in the morning."

"I'll do that, sir!" replied Slurk.

"Nothing must go wrong," continued Mr. Fingers. "There is a great deal at stake. I have much work to do destroying bridges and dams and freeways, and I can't let any cat get in my way!"

Mr. Fingers picked up a couple

"Nothing Must Go Wrong!"

of ball bearings and squeezed them flat.

"That's what I'll do to that cat if he gets in my way!" he said. "I will not tolerate any interference!"

"I understand, sir!" said Slurk. "I'll make sure that he won't bother you again!"

"He Won't Bother You Again!"

Worried Discussion

CHAPTER 7

A STICKY SITUATION

Tom and Jerry were back home discussing the events of the day.

"I still think we should go down to Chief McMinion and tell him about the things we've learned," said Tom.

"Don't be silly!" Jerry said. "I think he'd throw you out!"

"I don't think so," replied Tom. "Not after he hears what we have to say."

"I still think he'll throw you out!" Jerry said emphatically.

"We'll see," Tom answered.

They went down to see Chief McMinion and as Jerry predicted he was furious.

"You back again?" he exploded. "I thought I told you never to come here again!"

"I'm sorry, Chief," said Tom. "But I think I have some information for you."

"You Back Again?"

"What kind of information?" the chief stormed. "It had better be good!"

"It is," replied Tom. "There's a character called Mr. Fingers who is going to sabotage the whole city."

"You're crazy!" rumbled the chief.

"I'm not either," huffed Tom. "I saw a list of things that Mr. Fingers is planning to destroy. Freeways, railroads, bridges, dams!"

"That's right, Chief," added Jerry. "I saw the list, too. And do you know how he's going to do it?"

Tom Explains

"No!" growled the chief.

"With his *bare hands!*" said Jerry.

Chief McMinion turned red in the face.

"That's enough!" he shouted. "You two have been watching too many TV shows. GET OUT!"

Tom and Jerry got out before they could be thrown out. As they walked down the street they racked their brains trying to figure out what to do next.

"We can't let Mr. Fingers get away with all that sabotage. It's

"What Next?"

our patriotic duty to stop him," said Tom.

"I know," replied Jerry. "What can we do about it, though? He's a tough character."

"I'll think of something!" said Tom. "Don't forget—I'm F.E.L.I.N.E.!"

"How can I forget it?" muttered Jerry. "You keep reminding me of it all the time!"

"Next question," Jerry continued. "How can we stop Mr. Fingers?"

"He has to be stopped!" said

"Don't Forget—I'm F.E.L.I.N.E.!"

Tom. "He's out to destroy the whole city.'"

"And maybe the entire country!" added Jerry. "But how do we stop him?"

"Like I said, I'll come up with an answer!" responded Tom. "Just don't forget, I'm—"

"Yeah, I know," answered Jerry. "F.E.L.I.N.E."

"Thanks!" said Tom. "I knew you would understand."

"You're welcome!" said Jerry. "But you aren't solving our problem. We had better do something

"But We Still Have a Problem!"

about Mr. Fingers pretty rapidly or he'll get completely out of hand."

"What can we do?" asked Tom. "He's awfully clever!"

"You'll think of something," said Jerry. "After all, you're—"

"Yes, I know," responded Tom. "I'm F.E.L.I.N.E., and I'm going to solve this case if it's the last thing I do!"

"It might be the last thing *we* do unless we stop Mr. Fingers," said Jerry. "I have a feeling that he's after you and will stop at nothing!"

Troubled Twosome

They walked along the street, lost in thought. Suddenly Jerry stopped.

"Ugh!" he said.

"What's wrong?" Tom asked.

"I got my foot stuck in some old bubble gum somebody threw away!" answered Jerry.

Jerry pulled at his foot and Tom pulled at Jerry. It took the combined efforts of both of them to free his foot from the sticky stuff.

"Why can't people be more careful about where they throw their gum!" grumbled Jerry.

Sticky Situation

"That sure was sticky," commented Tom.

"That gives me an idea!" Jerry shouted.

"About what?" asked Tom.

"About how to trap Mr. Fingers!" replied Jerry.

"I'm listening," said Tom.

"This sticky, gooey bubble gum!" said Jerry. "You saw the way that it stuck to my feet? Maybe it would stick to Mr. Fingers' hands in the same way!"

"And how do you expect to get him all stuck up?" asked Tom.

Jerry Has an Idea

"I really don't know," answered Jerry. "We'll just have to wait for the right opportunity."

"That opportunity may never come," said Tom. "Maybe we'd better make our own!"

"What do you mean?" asked Jerry.

"Maybe we can lure Mr. Fingers into a trap!" Tom answered.

"How?" Jerry asked.

"I'll think of something!" replied Tom confidently. "Mr. Fingers may be smart, but every crook has a weak spot."

A Plan Takes Shape

"Listen to This!"

CHAPTER 8

A PLOT IS HATCHED

Upon arriving back home, Tom set to work thinking of a way to trap Mr. Fingers. He paced the floor for hours. Suddenly he stopped. An idea had finally come to him.

"Listen to this!" he exclaimed.
"I'm listening," Jerry said.

"Suppose we send him a note about a shipment of top secret supplies that will be in a boxcar parked on a railroad siding. We'll have the police there, and when he shows up we'll catch him red-handed," said Tom.

"What makes you think he'll fall for that?" asked Jerry.

"What have we got to lose?" replied Tom.

"Nothing but our necks, if all doesn't go right!" answered Jerry.

So they set to work composing a note to Mr. Fingers. It said:

Composing the Note

A box with top secret instruments will be in a boxcar parked on a railroad siding at Western Junction tomorrow.

                A Friend

"That should do it!" said Tom as he put the note in an envelope and sealed it.

"Suppose it doesn't?" asked Jerry.

"In that case, I'll think of some other plan to catch him," answered Tom confidently.

"Good luck!" said Jerry.

Tom got himself a big wooden

Tom Seals the Envelope

box and printed on it TOP SECRET MATERIAL—HANDS OFF! He then loaded it with a lot of junk, and he and Jerry took the box to Western Junction. There they put it in an empty boxcar standing on the siding.

"There's the bait for our trap," Tom chuckled. "Now all we have to do is mail this note. Then we'll go down and tell Chief McMinion about this clever plan."

"I just hope he doesn't throw you out again," muttered Jerry.

They went down to Headquarters

Bait for the Trap

and, as could have been expected, Chief McMinion wasn't overjoyed at seeing them.

Tom took a deep breath and explained his plan to the chief.

Chief McMinion paced the floor for a few minutes, deep in thought. Finally he said, "All right! I'll go along with this harebrained scheme of yours. But, so help me, if nothing comes of it, I'll throw you in jail and toss away the key!"

"It'll work!" answered Tom.

"It had better!" snapped the chief. "Now, here's what we'll do.

The Chief Considers

Tomorrow, after we're sure that Fingers has the note, I'll stake out my men around the boxcar."

"Don't you worry about a thing, Chief," Tom assured him. "I'm sure that Mr. Fingers will fall for this hook, line, and sinker!"

"He'd better!" replied the chief. "Now get out of here! I've got some planning to do!"

"Okay, Chief, and . . ." began Tom.

"OUT!" shouted the chief.

They got out. There was no use pressing their luck. At least the

"Get Out of Here!"

chief had agreed to follow Tom's plan. They certainly didn't want to antagonize him now.

"What do we do next?" asked Jerry.

"We might as well go home. Tomorrow morning we'll go down to the railroad yards and wait for Mr. Fingers to show up," replied Tom.

"Suppose he doesn't?" said Jerry.

"He will!" replied Tom. "I just feel it in my bones!"

Heading for Home

Chief McMinion Waits

CHAPTER 9

F.E.L.I.N.E. FIASCO

The next day was overcast and gloomy, with a hint of rain in the air. Nevertheless, Tom and Jerry were determined to bring Mr. Fingers to justice if possible.

They set out early for the railroad yards. When they arrived Chief McMinion was already there.

"Well," he growled, "where's this saboteur of yours?"

"He'll show up, Chief. I'm sure he will!" assured Tom.

At that moment there was a rumble of thunder, and rain began to come down in torrents. In no time Tom, Jerry, and the chief were drenched to the skin. Wet and miserable, they watched for a sign of Mr. Fingers. There was none.

"I must have been ten kinds of idiot for falling for this plan," grumbled the chief. Then he sneezed. "I'm catching cold on top

A Wet Watch

of it! We're going back."

Just then Tom noticed a furtive figure about to climb into the boxcar.

"Look, Chief!" he whispered excitedly. "There he is, just like I told you!"

The chief quickly got out his gun and they all hurried over to the boxcar.

"Throw up your hands!" demanded the chief.

"D-Don't shoot," said the man. "I'm just a poor old tramp. All I wanted was to get in out of the

"Look!"

rain and dry off a bit."

"Is this your Mr. Fingers?" Chief McMinion asked Tom.

"Well, uh, er . . ." Tom faltered. He had to admit that this man was about half the size and twice as old as Mr. Fingers. "I—I guess not!"

"ACHOO!" sneezed the chief. "I'm catching my death of cold!"

"I'm sorry, Chief," said Tom.

"Not half as sorry as you'll be when you're in jail!" snarled the chief.

Tom and Jerry thought that it

Only a Tramp

might be a good idea to get out of there before the chief made good his threat. He was about to make a grab for them when he gave out with another big sneeze. That gave Tom and Jerry a chance to run off. They didn't like to cross the chief, but they thought they could do more good outside of jail than inside. Eventually the chief would get over his anger.

They arrived at home wondering what they were going to do to stop Mr. Fingers without the help of the police. If they didn't stop

"Ka-choo!"

him, he would follow his timetable and destroy the railroad bridge.

In astonishment they gaped at the hulking figure in their doorway—Slurk! They turned, ready to run.

"Don't be alarmed!" Slurk purred. "I want to be your friend. Mr. Fingers and I just had an argument because I no longer approve of what he is doing."

Tom and Jerry looked at each other wonderingly. Could Slurk be on the level?

"What do you want from us?"

A Surprise Visitor

asked Tom suspiciously.

"I know how you can trap Mr. Fingers," replied Slurk. "All you have to do is follow my instructions."

"And what are *they*?" asked Jerry.

Slurk looked around carefully, as if to make sure no one else was listening.

"Do you know the old railroad trestle at Gloomy Gulch, north of town?" he asked.

Tom and Jerry agreed they did.

"Very well," said Slurk. "Meet

Slurk Gives Instructions

me there at exactly nine o'clock tomorrow morning and I will have some very important information for you."

With that he left. Tom and Jerry looked at each other.

"What do you think?" asked Tom.

"I'm not sure," replied Jerry. "He could be on the level about wanting to stop Mr. Fingers. Then again, he could be faking."

"Maybe he's figuring on some sort of reward," ventured Tom. "Anyway, I'm willing to take a

Tom and Jerry Watch

chance. What have we got to lose?"

"Nothing but our necks!" replied Jerry. "But if you're set on going, I guess I'll tag along!"

"That's the spirit!" said Tom. "I feel I'm doing the right thing!"

"I'm Doing the Right Thing!"

An Early Start

CHAPTER 10

TRESTLE TROUBLE

The next morning they set out bright and early for their meeting with Slurk. Jerry still had doubts about the whole thing.

"Don't you think we should at least tell Chief McMinion about it?" he asked Tom. "Maybe he's over being mad at us by now."

"I doubt it," said Tom. "He was pretty burned up! I don't think he'd believe a thing we told him. Nope, F.E.L.I.N.E. is going to have to do this by himself!"

"Just the same, I'm going to call the chief and tell him all about this!" said Jerry stubbornly. "Stop at a phone booth!"

Tom sighed. Why did he have to have such a suspicious little partner?

"Okay," he said. "But I don't think it will do any good!"

Tom dialed the number for

A Call to the Chief

Jerry, who couldn't reach the telephone, and Jerry spoke to the chief. Tom was right. The chief exploded and almost blew the phone off the wall.

"See?" said Tom. "What did I tell you?"

Crestfallen, Jerry joined Tom and they continued on their way. Soon they were at the old trestle at Gloomy Gulch.

It was a dark and forbidding place, and for the first time Tom had the feeling he shouldn't have come. However, he couldn't turn

At Gloomy Gulch Trestle

back now. They had come too far.

They made their way to the bottom of the gulch. There was no one in sight. The only sound was the huge timbers of the trestle creaking in the wind.

"L-Let's get out of here, Tom," stammered Jerry. "I don't like this!"

"Maybe Slurk changed his mind," Tom said. "I wouldn't blame him."

"Well, if he doesn't show up in ten seconds, I'm for getting out of here!" Jerry replied nervously,

A Spooky Spot

and he began to count. "One...two
...three...four...five...six...
seven...eight...nine...*ten!* Let's
go!"

"What's your hurry, gentlemen?" said a voice behind them.
"I always keep my appointments!"

They turned to see Slurk.

"Er, what's the information you
have?" asked Tom nervously.

"I'll let my master explain,"
answered Slurk. "He will arrive
at any moment."

Then they noticed that Slurk was
carrying a rope. And behind him

"What's Your Hurry?"

Mr. Fingers was approaching. They realized the whole business was a trap. What fools they'd been!

"My secret agent friend," said Mr. Fingers, "you've become a pest and a threat to my plans, so I'm afraid I must eliminate you."

Jerry managed to slip away unnoticed while Slurk was tying Tom to one of the trestle girders.

"Wh-what are you going to do?" Tom stammered.

"Give you an example of the power of my fingers," answered Mr. Fingers.

Tom Is Trapped

He took hold of a girder between two fingers and bent it slightly.

"How do you like that, friend?" he gloated. "In a few minutes the whole trestle will come down on you!"

While Mr. Fingers was occupied bending girders, and Slurk was watching the fun, Jerry managed to sneak behind Tom and loosen the rope.

The trestle began to sway and a section of it crashed down nearby.

"It's going!" cried Mr. Fingers.

The Trestle Starts to Go

"Let's get out of here!"

As Mr. Fingers and Slurk ran for safety, Tom managed to get loose. Both he and Jerry ran in the opposite direction, unnoticed by Slurk or Mr. Fingers.

The trestle swayed and creaked more and more, and suddenly fell with a tremendous crash.

Mr. Fingers rubbed his hands. "I guess that takes care of our snoopy friend!" he said.

"I just remembered that the cat had a small friend with him," said Slurk.

Narrow Escape

"No need to worry about him," Mr. Fingers replied confidently. "He will have been crushed along with that snoopy cat. Now we are free to resume the rest of our sabotage plans. Let us go and reconnoiter the dam."

Meanwhile, Tom and Jerry were losing no time in getting out of the gully.

"Boy!" Tom gasped. "That's as close as I ever want to come to losing my nine lives!"

"I wish I could remember what

Mr. Fingers Gloats

was next on the list for sabotage," said Jerry.

"Well," answered Tom, "we can't exactly go back to Mr. Fingers' and look at that list again."

"Why not?" asked Jerry. "I could sneak in without anybody noticing me."

"Wow!" exclaimed Tom. "You're sure a glutton for punishment!"

"I think I can do it," answered Jerry. "Sometimes it pays to be a little guy."

They sneaked back to Mr. Fingers' house. Mr. Fingers and Slurk

Gluttons for Punishment

had already returned and were discussing the next job. Jerry climbed up onto the window ledge to listen as they talked.

Mr. Fingers squeezed a few ball bearings. "After five, when we have destroyed the dam above the city," he said, "our work here will be completed. Then we move on to a new location."

Jerry gasped. If the dam went, a large part of the city would be flooded. As he watched Mr. Fingers squeeze the ball bearings, he had a sudden inspiration. He hurriedly

Listening at the Window

got down from the window and pulled Tom aside.

"They're going to destroy the dam next," Jerry whispered. "But I think I have a way to capture Mr. Fingers before he can do that!"

"How?" Tom asked.

"Remember that awful, sticky bubble gum I stepped in the other day? Suppose Mr. Fingers got his hands tangled up in it!" Jerry chortled.

"And just how do you propose to do that?" Tom asked.

"I think I have an idea, but it

Jerry Has an Idea

will take tricky timing," answered Jerry. "I'll tell you about it at home!"

Safe at home, Jerry told Tom his plan.

"First," Jerry explained, "I'll have to get a whole wad of bubble gum—enough to make a ball about the size of a football!"

"Whew!" said Tom. "That's going to take some chewing! Makes my jaws sore to think about it!"

"Mine, too!" replied Jerry. "But it's our only chance to stop Mr. Fingers!"

The Plan Unfolds

"Then what?" asked Tom. "We just can't ask him to play football!"

"He's set to destroy the dam exactly at five o'clock this afternoon, so we'll have to work fast!" Jerry said.

"But what happens when he gets his hands stuck up?" Tom asked.

"That's where you come in," replied Jerry. "You go down to see Chief McMinion while I go over to the dam!"

"See the chief!" Tom exclaimed. "Nothing doing! He'd throw me in jail!"

"Nothing Doing!"

"That's part of it," said Jerry.

Tom was puzzled. "I don't get it!" he said, scratching his head.

"Simple!" said Jerry. "You make him so mad that he chases you—right up to the dam. And if we're lucky, I'll have Mr. Fingers' hands all stuck up by the time the police arrive!"

"And if you don't?" asked Tom.

Jerry grinned. "Well, I'll get out of there just as fast as my little legs can carry me!"

"It had better work!" said Tom. "Otherwise we're both dead ducks!"

Almost Convinced

Aching Jaws

CHAPTER 11

DAFFODIL DIVERSION

Tom and Jerry bought a huge sack of bubble gum and set about chewing it. They chomped and chomped and chomped. By the time they had their football-size mass, both had sore jaws.

Now that they had the huge wad of gum, the problem was how to mold it into shape without getting all stuck up themselves.

Tom came up with the idea of using a pair of greased rubber gloves and went to work molding the gooey mess.

Before long he had the stickiest football in the world.

"Wait till Mr. Fingers catches a forward pass with this thing!" laughed Jerry.

"But how are you going to carry this sticky mess?" asked Tom.

"I'll wrap it in waxed paper," replied Jerry. "Now we'd better

Tom Molds a Gum Ball

review what we're going to do so nothing will go wrong. What's your role?"

"I'm to go down and get Chief McMinion mad at me so he chases me up to the dam," replied Tom.

"Right!" agreed Jerry. "And with luck you'll get there just after I've thrown this to Mr. Fingers!"

The time was growing short, so Jerry carefully wrapped the gummy football in waxed paper. It made quite a load for little Jerry to lift, but somehow he managed. He knew that if he didn't, nobody

Quite a Load

could stop Mr. Fingers from destroying the whole country.

After wishing each other good luck, Tom left in his old jalopy to see Chief McMinion and Jerry started out for the dam. Much depended on the success of their timing.

When Jerry reached the dam there was no one in sight. He hid himself in some bushes at one end of the dam to wait. After all, he was a bit early, and he was glad to set the bubble gum football down for a while.

Jerry Hides in the Bushes

As he waited, he wondered how Tom would make out with the chief. If he was caught, all would be lost.

Suddenly he heard a car stop on the road at the other end of the dam. It was Mr. Fingers in his old gardener disguise.

Jerry's heart did a flip-flop. Mr. Fingers was early! Their time schedule was shot to pieces! Tom could not possibly get here in time!

While Jerry pondered what to do, he noticed to his surprise that Mr. Fingers didn't go to the dam, but went up the bank on the edge

Mr. Fingers in Disguise

of the reservoir and started watering the daffodils growing there.

Then Jerry remembered that Chief McMinion had told them that Mr. Fingers, alias J. Hamhock Hamstrung, had donated daffodils to be planted around the reservoir.

Apparently Mr. Fingers had come early to tend his flowers.

All Jerry could hope was that Mr. Fingers would take plenty of time caring for his daffodils. That would give Tom time to get here with Chief McMinion.

As Jerry watched, Mr. Fingers

Watering His Daffodils

finished watering the daffodils on the far side of the dam and started to walk across it.

"Oh, my gosh!" thought Jerry to himself. "This is it!"

But again to his surprise, Mr. Fingers continued across the dam and stopped near Jerry's hiding place.

Jerry thought the end had come and crouched farther under the bush. He wondered for a moment if he could throw the football right then and there and get out while he was still healthy.

A Nervous Jerry

But Mr. Fingers only wanted to water the daffodils which were on that side of the dam. He paused for a moment by the bush where Jerry was hidden and poured water over it.

Jerry got a complete drenching, but he didn't dare say a word or even shake off the water.

Mr. Fingers continued to water each daffodil with loving care. Luckily there were plenty of them for him to tend.

However, Jerry, drenched as he was, could no longer suppress a

Jerry Gets Sprinkled

sneeze. He gave out with a great big KACHOO!

Mr. Fingers paused and looked around. He started toward the bush where Jerry was hidden.

Jerry, terrified, crouched lower and lower as Mr. Fingers approached his hiding place.

The evil saboteur poked around the bush for a moment, but luckily it was so thick that both Jerry and his bubble gum football were effectively hidden. Finally Mr. Fingers grunted something to himself and moved off to resume his watering.

Jerry Sneezes

Jerry heaved a great sigh of relief. That had been a close one! He wondered how long his luck would last. There weren't too many flowers left to be watered, so probably in a few minutes Mr. Fingers would start destroying the dam.

Suddenly Jerry's alert ears heard the sound of footsteps. Someone was coming! He peeked out cautiously.

It was Slurk coming across the dam. Jerry hurriedly ducked back under the bush.

Slurk approached Mr. Fingers

Slurk Arrives

and said, "I'd like to remind you, sir, it's almost time to destroy the dam."

"I know! I know!" snapped Mr. Fingers. "But I must finish with my daffodils first! I spent many happy hours planting these beautiful flowers and I can't stand to see them neglected. The dam can wait."

"Very well, sir," replied Slurk.

Jerry again heaved a great sigh of relief. "Thank goodness for daffodils," he thought. "This will give Tom additional time."

"It's Almost Time, Sir!"

Mr. Fingers continued his watering, but Jerry started to chew his fingernails. The suspense was getting him.

Meanwhile, Tom reached the office of Police Chief McMinion.

"What, you back again?" the chief exploded. "What is it this time? Is somebody going to blow up City Hall?"

"No, sir," answered Tom meekly. "I just wanted to pay you a friendly visit."

Tom glanced at the clock on the

An Angry Chief

wall. There were still fifteen minutes to go before the dam was to be destroyed. He had to stall for a few more minutes before really irritating the chief.

"A friendly visit!" snorted the chief. "I've no time for that! Now get out of here before I have you thrown into jail! This is your last warning!"

Tom again glanced at the clock. His timing had to be right. He decided to make his move.

"Now don't get sore, Chiefie," he said. "I've got some real news for

Tom Stalls for Time

you this time. Honestly!"

The chief burned. "I warn you!" he said. "My patience is about at an end."

"Just hear me out," pleaded Tom. "My news is this: Your friend, J. Hamhock Hamstrung, otherwise known as Mr. Fingers, is going to destroy the dam this afternoon!"

"Now I know you've flipped," growled the chief. "I've told you before that J. Hamhock Hamstrung is one of our most respected citizens."

"You've Flipped!"

"If you don't believe me, come on out to the dam right now," said Tom. "He's going to make his move at five o'clock!"

"That does it!" snapped the chief. "I don't think it's safe for you to be roaming around! I'm going to lock you up and throw the key away! You've pestered me for the last time!"

"You'll have to catch me first!" laughed Tom.

The chief lunged at Tom, who started to run around the desk.

"McKimson! Connell! Craig!"

"You'll Have to Catch Me First!"

yelled the chief. "Help me catch this nut!"

As the men ran into the room Tom decided the time was *now* and ducked past them and ran out of the office.

"Stop or I'll shoot!" shouted the chief.

Tom hadn't reckoned with this possibility and he was about to stop when he thought of Jerry up at the dam all by himself. He decided to take a chance and keep on going. He jumped into his jalopy and headed for the dam.

"Stop or I'll Shoot!"

It wasn't long before the chief and his men were following in hot pursuit.

Tom knew that his old car would never be a match for the police car and only hoped he had enough of a start to get to the dam before he was overtaken.

The Plan Was Working

Mr. Fingers Gets Ready

CHAPTER 12

A MESSY MISSILE

At the dam, Mr. Fingers finally finished watering his daffodils.

"Well, Slurk," announced Mr. Fingers, "I guess it's time for us to make our move!"

"About time!" muttered Slurk.

Mr. Fingers went to the center of the dam, leaned over, and broke off a piece of concrete with his fingers.

"Look, Slurk!" he gloated. "This will be a cinch!"

Jerry watched in amazement as Mr. Fingers broke off more pieces of the dam.

"It shouldn't take long at this rate, sir!" remarked Slurk.

"It won't," answered Mr. Fingers. "All I have to do is start the water flowing over!"

As Jerry watched, he wondered what was keeping Tom. It looked like Mr. Fingers would have the dam demolished in no time. Could

"This Will Be a Cinch!"

it be that Chief McMinion had thrown Tom into jail? If so, all would be lost.

Suddenly, in the distance, came the sound of a siren. Mr. Fingers stopped.

"What's that?" he asked in alarm.

"Oh, nothing, sir!" answered Slurk. "Probably the police chasing some speeder!"

The sound of the siren grew louder. Jerry was exalted. Tom had done his part. It wouldn't be long now.

"What's That?"

"They're coming this way!" exclaimed Mr. Fingers. "I've got to work fast!"

His fingers tore at the concrete, and the breach in the dam widened.

Just then, Tom's car screeched to a halt. The chief's car stopped right behind it.

"This is it!" said Jerry as he ran from under the bush. "Catch!" He threw the bubble gum football at the astonished Mr. Fingers.

Mr. Fingers instinctively threw up his hands to catch the missile. In no time he was completely ensnared

"Catch!"

in the inextricable mess.

The more he struggled, the more tangled he became. This was a problem not even his powerful fingers could cope with. Soon he was a helpless, sticky mess.

At that moment Tom came running up, followed by Chief McMinion.

"There's your man, Chief!" said Tom. "Now do you believe me?"

"Yes!" put in Jerry. "With my own eyes I saw him try to demolish the dam!"

The perplexed chief didn't know

A Snarled Saboteur

what to do for a moment. Then he spotted Slurk trying to sneak off, and he sprang into action.

"Stop that man!" he ordered.

Slurk was soon nabbed.

"I had nothing to do with it! It was all his idea!" he whined, pointing at Mr. Fingers.

"Is that true?" the chief demanded of the helpless Mr. Fingers.

Mr. Fingers said nothing for a moment, then finally sighed. "Yes, I did it. But if you must take me in, please make sure someone takes care of my daffodils."

"It Was His Idea."

"We will," the chief assured him. Then he turned to Tom and Jerry. "I guess I owe you boys an apology. I was wrong about you."

"Aw, shucks, Chief, that's okay," said Tom. "We all make mistakes!"

The Chief Apologizes

Heroes of the Hour

CHAPTER 13

A NEW START

And so the case of the mysterious saboteur, Mr. Fingers, was solved.

Tom and Jerry were the heroes of the hour. They got their names in the papers and were invited to the mayor's office for commendation.

Jerry modestly disclaimed any credit for solving the case and said that Tom—or rather, F.E.L.I.N.E.—had done it all by himself.

Just as the mayor was about to hang a medal around Tom's neck, Tom blinked his eyes and found himself right back in his own chair at home! He realized it had all been a dream. But what a dream! It was one he'd never forget.

On television, the Bombsie Wombsies commercial was just ending.

"Ha, ha!" laughed Jerry. "You fell asleep during the commercial! And, boy, did you snore!"

Only a Dream

"Wait till I tell you about the dream I had!" exclaimed Tom. "I was a secret agent and solved a big crime!"

"Speaking of secret agents," said Jerry, "this package of Bombsie Wombsies has an Instant Trench Coat that you make by just adding water!"

"Swell!" replied Tom. "Maybe I can wear that and at least pretend to be a secret agent!"

Jerry poured the concoction into a bowl, added water, and started stirring. After a few minutes he

Jerry Experiments

announced that it was ready, reached into the bowl, and pulled out—not a full-size trench coat, but a mouse-size one!

"Oh, goody!" exclaimed Jerry. "I can pretend to be a secret agent!"

So Jerry, dressed in his new trench coat, sat down to watch the conclusion of the adventures of Secret Agent 67⅞. And Tom, just a bit envious of the new coat, sat down beside him.

Tom had had his adventure. Now it was Jerry's turn.

A New Secret Agent

Other BIG LITTLE BOOKS® Available

BATMAN—The Cheetah Caper

*** BUGS BUNNY**—Accidental Adventure

BUGS BUNNY—Double Trouble on Diamond Island

*** BUGS BUNNY**—The Last Crusader

DONALD DUCK—The Fabulous Diamond Fountain

*** DONALD DUCK**—The Lost Jungle City

DONALD DUCK—Luck of the Ducks

*** DONALD DUCK**—Volcano Valley

THE FANTASTIC FOUR—The House of Horrors

GRIMM'S GHOST STORIES

LASSIE—Adventure in Alaska

LASSIE—Old One-Eye

* With "FLIP-IT" cartoons

LASSIE—The Shabby Sheik

THE LONE RANGER Outwits Crazy Cougar

MICKEY MOUSE—Adventure in Outer Space

MICKEY MOUSE—Mystery at Disneyland

* **THE PINK PANTHER**—Adventure in Z-Land

POPEYE—Danger, Ahoy!

POPEYE—Ghost Ship to Treasure Island

* **POPEYE**—Queen Olive Oyl

* **ROAD RUNNER**—The Super Beep-Catcher

TOM AND JERRY Meet Mr. Fingers

TWEETY AND SYLVESTER—The Magic Voice

WOODY WOODPECKER—The Meteor Menace

* With "FLIP-IT" cartoons

GOLDEN® *Full-Length Adventures*

- ALGONQUIN
- THE CALL OF THE WILD
- DR. JEKYLL AND MR. HYDE
- FRANKENSTEIN
- GOLDEN PRIZE
- LASSIE – four exciting adventures
- SEVEN GREAT DETECTIVE STORIES
- SHERLOCK HOLMES
- SHUDDERS
- TALES OF TIME AND SPACE
- TEE-BO AND THE PERSNICKETY PROWLER
- TEE-BO IN THE GREAT HORT HUNT
- THAT'S OUR CLEO
- THE WAR OF THE WORLDS